THE DAY THE DONKEY FLEW

Five Natural Resources for Inspired Living

Elisa C. Newsome Smith

Elisa's Playshop   Miami, Florida
2013

This book is a work of fiction.

Published by Elisa's Playshop
www.elisasplayshop.com

Illustrations: Shift Wood
Cover design and interior layout: Tamian Wood, Beyond Design
International. www.BeyondDesignInternational.com

ISBN 978-0-9892716-0-8

Dedication

To donkeys waiting to take flight
and
To Dr. Manuel R. Gomez as he soars

Acknowledgment

To the Universe for the possibility of flight

Prologue

Back in the time when days were filled with arduous, long hours of work and nights marked by dullness and exhaustion lived the Richardson Family.

The clan of six brothers, their wives and children farmed and raised cattle. Wrestling all day with Mother Nature left everyone too tired to dream, too drained to take on the impossible.

Everyone, that is, except the children of Joseph, the youngest brother. His daughters, Joy, Hope, Rose, Faith and Grace, dreamed, defied impossibilities and even believed donkeys could fly.

This is their story.

1

Joy makes donkeys want to fly

"Ha.....ha......ha," uttered the arriving baby.

No one present at the birth knew what it meant. Could it be that the newborn had difficulty breathing?

As the baby stretched out into the new world, the sound became more of a rapturous "hah, hah, hah." But what did that peculiar sound mean? Bewilderment settled on the father, doctor and the father's sister.

At the child's sounds, the fatigued mother, Isabel, rebounded with energy. She jumped out of the labor bed and grabbed her baby from the doctor.

"She's laughing," delighted Isabel as she spun around the room with the child nestled to her breast.

Laughing? Most babies cry when expelled from the comfort of their mothers' womb.

"Are you sure it's laughter?" queried Joseph, the father.

"No doubt about it. I know laughing when I hear it," beamed Isabel.

It had been a long time since laughter greeted the farm. With the current drought, last year's locust infestation and the crop-freezing winter the previous year, the farming family had plenty to cry about, but not much to laugh at.

Now, to the amazement of all those present, the infant chuckled as if to say, "glad to be here."

And although Joseph had hoped for a son, his disappointment gave way to the broadness of his daughter's smile and those delightful giggling sounds. For the first time in recent memory, he, too, bent over with laughter.

Joy, literally, had been born on the farm.

2

Joseph's taxing days seemed kinder and shorter with the birth of Joy. He eased through his chores. The ground didn't fight as he plowed it. The dirt just parted on its own.

The oranges willingly embraced his hand, no plucking or pulling. Nor did he need to climb the ladder for those reaching the heavens. Oranges just fell from the sky. And not a one bruised as they tumbled to his feet.

Joseph didn't mind the wild rabbits munching on his carrots and cabbages as much. Where before he would spend hours setting traps, Joseph now shrugged it off, more than happy to share his bounty.

His mind consumed all day with images of Joy, Joseph felt stronger at the end of his work. The grind of earning a living no longer bested the farmer.

Joy's influence permeated the farm. The baby forever wore a smile that made others want to smile as well. No one was immune to Joy's charm. All Joseph's stoic brothers and their sour-faced wives agreed that they just couldn't help feeling giddy when they looked into the face of the delightful child.

And in all her days, Joy never cried or fussed. When hungry, she'd chuckle and a hearty howl meant "feed me now." A snicker indicated Joy desired a clean diaper.

Joy's antics energized Isabel, making it a delight to attend to her needs.

3

With the arrival of Joy, lightness settled over the place. The daily atmosphere vibrated with music and singing, something previously reserved only for Sunday worship gatherings.

The grim families started seeing more humor in things. Everyone laughed when birds plucked the fruit-decorated hat off the head of the wife of Matthew, one of Joseph's brothers.

The wife wore the garish hat topped with fake oranges and purple grapes, like the Crown of England. As she moved with a purpose on the way to Sunday services, a couple of black crows swooped down and flew off with the hat.

Before Joy, no one would have dared to laugh at such indignity. But now, after Joy, the husband, children and even the victim of the crows' caper laughed until their bellies ached.

Inspiration also accompanied Joy's birth. Isabel started painting. Prior to delivering Joy, her only fulfillment had been duty, days tending to the home and helping with the farm chores.

With Joy, her hands twirled in radiant hues of green, yellow, blue, orange and pink. They danced across the canvas with no hint that hours earlier they had been tools for milking the cow, pulling weeds from the vegetable patch and pushing sewing needles through rugged denim to mend her husband's overalls.

Isabel's newfound creativity showed up as meadows of wildflowers. Running vines of violets, wispy dandelions adrift in the breeze and lilies of all colors bursting forth to proclaim "good morning" found stardom on her canvas.

"Honey, where did these paintings come from?" Joseph asked when he found a stack underneath the dining table.

"I painted them," she answered.

"You painted them?" he puzzled? "I didn't know you could paint."

"I didn't either," she replied. "I just felt it."

Joseph noted that the house always sparkled, he never missed a hearty meal, Joy had fresh diapers, and a bounty of homemade soap and cans of preserved vegetables and fruits stocked the kitchen shelves, and he asked in astonishment, "When did you find the time and energy to paint?"

"I just did," Isabel replied with a smile of deep contentment.

4

Hope makes donkeys believe they can fly

In addition to the ability to paint, Isabel realized another gift.

Reflections of realities yet to come crept into her sleep as her imagination awakened.

People in the Richardson Family didn't dream.

Between breaking dirt, battling the weather and backing down crop-and cattle-threatening diseases, they lacked the dreamlike, stimulating energy that created night visions. Sleep overcame them like a heavy, suffocating mass that rendered them unconscious the moment the body hit the bed. Inspiration couldn't penetrate the darkness.

Besides being too tired, they had no motivation to fantasize. Wealthy in land and the prominence

of supplying the entire county with beef and vegetables, the brothers proudly stood in stature on
their inheritance.

Wishful longings didn't disturb Isabel's sleep.
Her imagery portrayed no hint of desire for anything, nor wishes to be anyone or anywhere else.
Her dreams seemed to be messages, communications.

In the first scenario, Isabel envisioned a single
vine. A bud sprouted on the vine. It bloomed into
a white jasmine flower, so lifelike she could feel
the calmness of the sweet scent.

The dreamer understood the vision to hint at
reproduction. Should she expect the arrival of a
baby, Isabel wondered? But within a matter of
days, she knew her womb was not with child.
One of her sisters-in-law must have conceived.

For fear of ridicule, Isabel couldn't tell her family
that she had dreamt there would be an addition
to the clan. They didn't have encounters with the
imaginative and would have branded her as foolish for embracing such nonsense. Her people lived
off the land and only believed in that which they
could touch, tangible things that produced profits.

Worse than that, they would have thought that
her wild fancies must mean that her chores were
sorely neglected.

Without arousing suspicion, she went about
investigating which of her sisters-in-law might
be with child. She closely watched them, looking for signs of new life. None glowed or gained
weight, nor did any have trouble keeping their
breakfast down.

Had she given too much credibility to her power to see that which her eyes hadn't witnessed, Isabel wondered? Ruler of the world, creator of all life, only the Supreme Being had known who and what were to come.

God gave man the Bible to comprehend his ways, but neither Isabel nor her relatives had the acquaintance of anyone who knew the Almighty intimately, his thoughts and desires.

The Lord expressed his sentiment through blessings and curses. A bountiful harvest meant the Almighty had been pleased, his ways observed. Calamity signaled a displeased God, whose wrath wielded hardship and disastrous weather.

The family's response to the Supreme Being took the form of placating and beseeching prayers and worship services courting his good graces.

The thought of the possibility of God being the transmitter of her dreams unnerved Isabel. Who was she to have had the Lord's confidence? How arrogant of her to believe that she knew God's will, had seen his soul.

Knowing only farming, Isabel reached the sobering conclusion that she did not have the intelligence to receive divine communications. She had not been dealing with the Almighty; her mind merely reeled with worry about the crops. "Stop fretting, the harvest will be bountiful," Isabel figured her faculties had conveyed through the image of the blooming vine.

A couple of weeks later, Isabel had another impression in which she was weeding in the garden when a bundle fell from the sky and into her hands. She opened the parcel which contained a baby. The child spoke the word, "believe."

5

A month had passed since Isabel's conception of the talking baby and she found herself two weeks late. Given the state of her cycle, Isabel had become receptive to the realm of dreams, not fearing their origin. Something or someone had been communicating with her. Not feeling nauseous or tightness in her belly, Isabel was unable to justify her belief and kept her thoughts of expectancy to herself.

She quietly carried out her normal activities, fighting urges to share her thoughts. Isabel's insights refused to be suppressed. While painting, her brush strokes didn't take the shape of flowers as customary. Instead, an infant crawling through an open field appeared on the canvas.

Although she lacked any signs of pregnancy, the painting confirmed Isabel's suspicion. That evening she showed the artwork to her husband.

"A baby, I sure hope it's a boy," was Joseph's only reply.

That night as Isabel slept, the world turned pink. Rays of washed out red emitted from the sky as the sun sported pink. A mass of pink replaced fields that once exploded with green, yellow, purple and orange flora. Butterflies with wings dipped in pink frosting fluttered around her front door.

Again, Isabel didn't share with her husband the ethereal communication, which she interpreted to mean the expectancy of a daughter. Why dash his hopes when dreams don't necessarily materialize?

That night she had another visit from the talking baby who told Isabel, "My name is Hope."

Six months later the child arrived and Joseph continued hoping for a boy.

6

Rose lifts donkeys when they fall from the sky

A month after Hope's birth, Isabel had a recurrence of the vine-vision.

A single vine with a bounty of vibrant green leaves teeming with white blooms of jasmine appeared. The vine thrived. Isabel believed that it represented her daughter Joy.

A year old, Joy had begun walking and speaking a few words, including "Mommy" and "Daddy." Her favorite phrase was "baby happy." If you asked her if she wanted to eat, she'd answer "baby happy." Did she need a fresh diaper? "Baby happy" the toddler replied. When her father returned from the fields, Joy greeted him with "baby happy."

A second thriving vine manifested. Jasmine petals dangled everywhere, reassurance that

Hope would do just as well as her sister.

Then a third vine emerged. It had no flowers, and just a couple of leaves. A bud sprung forth and started to open. Before it could fully bloom, the bud closed and the vine quickly dissipated.

A novice in dealing with psychic phenomena, Isabel found herself bewildered by the dried-up vine. She failed to perceive its foreboding implications. That it told of her third pregnancy and a harsh growing season.

There would be lightning strikes and fire engulfing the cornfields. And Isabel, well into her pregnancy, had to battle the blazes along with the rest of the family. A tornado that uprooted many trees followed the fire, and again Isabel was employed to gather any salvageable fruit.

The catastrophic weather, coupled with caring for two young infants depleted Isabel. Her weakened body ejected the developing child before term. Isabel delivered seven weeks premature.

Dead silence filled the room. Curled up and hard, the baby came into the world lifeless. Gloom hung in the air. The doctor called for a sack cloth to wrap the lifeless infant.

"Maybe it was for the best, it was just another girl," Joseph consoled himself.

But Isabel rejected comfort. She keened with agonizing wails as they tried to pry the cold child from her chest. It took nearly twelve minutes for them to pull the infant from her. Hot tears of determination fell from Isabel's eyes onto the baby as she lost her grip.

The doctor laid the blue baby on the dresser and gathered the sack cloth. But before he could put the stillborn into the bag, the stone of flesh began to rise and fall, rise and fall, rise and fall.

She was breathing. In disbelief, they gasped as the infant bloomed.

They named her Rose.

7

Faith empowers donkeys to fly

Joseph abandoned his faith and gave up hope for a Joseph Jr. ever inhabiting the farm. It had been two years since his wife gave birth to Rose and there was no twinkle of a son in her eyes.

Wanting and effort were simply not enough. After tending to the business of farming, the wishful father ended his days with the business of child-making. Whether in the mood or not, Joseph and Isabel daily tried for a male heir. When their labor bore no fruit, they summoned the prayer warriors.

Now, the convention of prayer ushered in and escorted out the day.

Everyone thanked the Lord for waking them in the morning and thanked Him again in the evening for keeping them safe throughout their activities and for their many blessings. Times of impending doom — hurricanes, freezing weather, droughts, canker outbreaks among the crops and animals and so on — called the prayer warriors into action.

The prayer warriors consisted of all the farmers' wives who convened three times a day for hours at a time pleading with the Almighty to move on their behalf. Singing, dancing, praising his wonderful name and even some crying were all utilized to influence the stars to line up in their favor.

In addition to divine Intervention, Joseph and Isabel resorted to other fertility remedies. After all, faith without works was foolish. They consulted the doctor and modified their meals.

The couple's traditional diet of plenty of beans, peas, nuts, fruits and vegetables contained the ingredients for reproduction. Given the situation, imported oysters topped salads of spinach, purple onions and red and green peppers. Isabel drank milk laced with ground flaxseed. A high-priced turkey, normally invited to the dinner table only on Thanksgiving Day, became a sacrifice.

Joseph made sacrifices as well, foregoing his three steaming cups of coffee in the morning and underwear. The young farmer had to go bare bottom. The family doctor explained that

Elisa C. Newsome Smith

Joseph's man parts needed to hang loose and breathe.

After a few months, Joseph wound up with a bottom as tender as a newborn's from the denim scratching his naked behind, but no baby.

8

The relentless longing for a male child had no bearing on Joseph's relationship with his three daughters. Appreciative of Joy, Hope and Rose, he knew his life had been enriched immeasurably by their presence.

Joy's smile continued to ease the strains of farm living. Gazes from Hope's deep, glistening eyes made Joseph and Isabel feel as if they were being transformed into something glorious. New life peered from her gaze.

During the times Joseph felt overwhelmed and lacked the strength to finish a task, he looked at Rose, a constant reminder to never give up.

When crops appeared to fail, he remembered that Rose, born dead, had bloomed.

He loved his daughters more than anyone knew. Survival had bred Joseph's desperation for a son. To be without a male heir jeopardized the family's future.

Inheritance rights excluded daughters, destined to marry and take their husbands' names, meaning that the farm would one day lose the Richardson moniker. Joseph had three older sisters, two nobody mentioned after they married and moved away. The third sister, Caroline, never wed. She had nothing to her name and lived with the help of her brothers.

With no one to carry on his name, Joseph feared his branch would wither.

9

Like the planting seasons, order reigned on the farm from summer to winter and back again. Summer squash seeds were embedded in the earth February through March and again August through September, sprouting profits in just over a month. The heat of late spring and summer stifled the growth of squash, and planting then reaped sinfulness, bearing no fruit.

The Richardsons revered the growing cycles just as they did the Holy Bible. Come February, the family planted sweet potatoes until June. Cabbage and broccoli seedlings covered the fall and winter. October and November belonged to sweet strawberries.

To adhere to the planting season, farmers had to know their place in the world. The clan lived in central Florida where tomatoes are planted from January through March and again in September. In south Florida, growers planted tomatoes from August through March.

Placement merited just as an important role in the Richardson Family. Birth order dictated position and possibilities.

Elder John they called John the first-born, denoting his status. Brother Number Two was everyone's nickname for Nathaniel, who was born second. Matthew, the fourth child but third among the males, answered to Brother Number Three. Following Matthew in birth, Jeremiah earned the epithet Brother Number Four.

Between Brother Number Five, Daniel, and Joseph were two sisters, Girl Child Number Two and Girl Child Number Three. Being the last child, Joseph eluded the destination of Brother Number Six. Instead, he was christened End of the Line.

Joseph deemed himself a victim of the curse of the youngest child. Not being the first-born, he had little to say regarding the affairs of the farm. Joseph had no say in where he lived, what he produced, and apparently he had no say in the gender of his offspring.

Since the death of their father, Elder John had been the leader of the family, overseeing all business matters and assigning duties. All decisions, including what crops to produce, responses to crises, and what was and wasn't allowed were dictated by Elder John, who also claimed the role of family minister.

God hadn't called Elder John. Tradition ordained him. Since the beginning, every first-born male held the responsibility for the family's salvation. And the custom ruled, never minding that Jeremiah, the fourth brother, had the gift for speaking words that soothed any ailing soul.

Day after day, Joseph had dirt in his face. From the time he was old enough to pluck vegetables from a vine, he toiled in the fields. If Joseph had been born first or even second, his life would not have been one of drudgery.

He would have been a cowboy, just like his father. From knee high Joseph tried to walk in the patriarch's boots. Awe-stricken, he twirled his father's lasso as he imagined himself high on a trusty steed.

"Yee haw," he yelled as images of heroic acts teased him. Joseph's heart pounded with adrenaline as he defended the herd from wild beasts.

Little Joseph wanted to grow up to be a cowboy and so did his brothers. Overseeing the cattle carried the distinction of being the choice job of the ranch and farm. The honor went to Elder John and Nathaniel, brothers born first and second.

Birth succession also dictated where you lived on the farm.

On the land stood three houses, one with twelve rooms, and two more with seven rooms each.

Elder John and his family lived in the largest house, a three-story structure of grandeur that was haunted with the legacy of no-nonsense men who found honor in living by their hands, men who fought and worked hard to secure the family's existence.

French cut-glass chandeliers hung from the ceilings in the foyer, sitting room, dining area and parlor. A rug dating back to the era of King George II graced the polished wood floor in the sitting room. The living room's mantle displayed first printings of the novels *Pamela: Virtue Rewarded* and *Clarissa: The History of a Young Lady* by Samuel Richardson, an English author believed to be a relative.

Large enough to hold an oak wood table that comfortably sat eighteen, the dining room still had room to place chairs for eight diners away from the table. A small ball with plenty of room for dancing and mingling could be held in the parlor, although it was primarily used as a sanctuary for Sunday worship services and other special gatherings.

Images of men with broad foreheads, squared jaws, and stony faces glared from the walls throughout the home. They were the family's patriarchs, men who ruled with tradition, the fear of God and the promise of hard work. Men of valor, they led their families through the hazardous pioneering days of Florida, through British and Spanish rule, through the Indian and Civil wars.

The family history started with Goddard Richardson and his wife Joanne. At the age of twenty the newlyweds left England in 1770 to start a new life in America. Goddard laid claim to six acres in central Florida, which he and his bride farmed.

Goddard found good fortune. His wife gave birth to two sons, Christopher and Ernest, and a daughter Sophie. His land grew from six acres to forty. As Goddard's cash crops brought in profits, he purchased cattle. He only suffered the loss of his youngest son Ernest, killed in a land dispute with other settlers.

Prosperity continued its friendship with the Richardson clan. Despite changes in government and war, they flourished in children, land and cattle. Christopher and his wife Elyse had five daughters and one son, Jonathan, who had three sons, Emmett, Frederick and Oswald.

Emmett and Frederick died in the war with the Indians. The surviving son, Oswald, mastered multiplication. The most proliferate of all the Richardson men, he fathered Joseph, his five brothers and three sisters. The farm contained one hundred and twenty acres and twenty cattle when Ozzie took over. Under his leadership, the Richardson Farm and Ranch boasted three hundred acres and forty-five cattle.

The Big House stood fifty yards in front of the other two houses, which were side by side. Brothers Two and Three shared one of the two houses and Brothers Four and Five lived in the other. Modest and functional, the structures belied the family's riches.

Prior to marriage, Joseph lived with Elder John in the Big House, reserved for the patriarch and any unmarried siblings. When Joseph married, he and his bride found no room in the other two family homes.

An old barn near the grazing fields of the cattle had been converted into a two-bedroom house with a kitchen and eating area for the youngest brother and his wife. Discounting the smell of the neighboring livestock, the newlyweds considered the accommodation cozy.

At least five acres stood between Joseph's home and his brothers. The distance typified the youngest brother's relationship with his siblings. Being born last, he always felt isolated. More than fifteen years separated End of the Line and Elder John.

Being last in line cost Joseph his childhood fantasy of being a cowboy, occupancy in the family residence and he believed an heir.

His brothers started reproducing before Joseph developed an interest in mating. By the time Joseph married, Elder John and Brother Number Two had three sons each, Brother Number Three had five, including a set of twins, Brother Number Four had two, and Brother Number Five had one son. Even his married sisters had borne their husbands a batch of boys.

Joseph figured that when it came time for him to breed, the family had used up its allotment of boys.

The order of his birth truly prophesied the End of the Line.

10

Isabel, too, succumbed to her husband's belief that they had seen the last of their blessed events.

Not that she needed any more children. Her heart swelled with satisfaction from raising Joy, Hope and Rose and tending to her family's needs.

Joseph's distress, however, caused her consternation. Besieged with the pressure to conceive a male child, Isabel sometimes lost sight of her completeness.

Gone were the idyllic sceneries that inspired her paintings. Sleep didn't refresh her. Dreams of budding vines and talking babies evaded Isabel. No visions of any kind came during the days or nights.

She, too, had lost faith.

In her anguish, she didn't follow Hope when her daughter spoke, "Mommy, we need another bed."

She dismissed her, "The bed you have is big enough for you and Joy."

"It's not for us," Hope replied.

Preoccupied with her husband's gloom, Isabel couldn't hear Hope. Nor did she realize that it had been nearly two months since she had her cycle.

Another six weeks passed before Isabel finally realized that she could be with child and remembered Hope's request for another bed.

Unable to dream herself, she called for the three-year-old Hope.

"Sweetie, why did you ask Mommy for another bed?"

"The baby needs a place to sleep," replied Hope.

"Rose can still sleep in the cot until she gets bigger," Isabel replied. "We'll move her bed out of Mommy and Daddy's room into the room with you and Joy."

"No Mommy," Hope said. "Rose will sleep with me, and Joy needs a bed."

"Ok, Joy can sleep on the cot and you and Rose can have the bed," offered Isabel.

"The baby needs the cot," answered Hope.

"Hope, there is no other baby besides Rose," said Isabel.

"Oh yes there is, Mommy," Hope said confirming Isabel's suspicion that she could be pregnant.

Eager to know how and what Hope knew about the baby, she questioned the child. "Hope, how do you know there's another baby?"

"I saw the baby," Hope said.

Afraid of the answer, Isabel wanted to know to the baby's gender.

"What did the baby look like Hope?" asked Isabel nervously.

"A baby," answered Hope.

Heart about to explode from her chest, Isabel could barely get the words out, "Was it a boy baby or girl baby?" fretted Isabel.

"Mommy, it was just a baby," Hope replied.

"Oh just a baby," sighed a fretful Isabel, not wanting to suffer her husband's anguish if the child was not the long-awaited heir.

"Mommy, the baby said that you must have faith," Hope added.

Hope had taken over the role of dreamer. A child claimed Isabel's womb and heart. And just as Hope commanded, Isabel did have faith.

Faith, the fourth daughter, arrived on the farm five months later.

11

Grace flies donkeys

Joseph and his wife had given up the idea of trying for a son. Bearing Faith took too much out of them. The endless prayers ceased, the special diets and herbs didn't make the menu, and cotton undergarments tightly secured the family jewels.

The couple had four lovely daughters. Faith now six months old already showed signs that she would prosper. In the first month of her life, the infant rolled over. She demonstrated tremendous neck and arm strength as she raised her body and flipped back and forth. Long before expected, Faith crawled. At four months she started chasing after her three sisters as if she had been designated "It" in a game of tag.

Gratefulness overtook Joseph as he watched over his healthy, thriving daughters. He stopped worrying about their futures and his place in the family. The angst of needing an heir subsided.

So enraptured in their current baby, Isabel had been expecting for four full months by the time she realized the presence of Grace, the couple's fifth daughter.

12

Five Years Later

Maybe it's because she hadn't been planned, Grace knew the gift of Life. She didn't owe her being to the will of parents. Life simply begot life.

Life gives itself to trees, to birds, and Life had given itself to her.

Life freely gave in Grace's eyes. She didn't understand the strenuous labors of her Daddy and uncles. After all, Life had produced the crops and animals.

She really didn't understand why she and her sisters only received gifts and treats on special occasions – birthdays, Christmas, and when they made good grades (A's and B's) in school.

"Daddy, why can't we have cake every

day?" Grace asked."It wouldn't be special if we had cake every day," Joseph said.

"But Daddy, every day is special," Grace said.

Specialness, indeed, characterized Joseph's life. The most beautiful beings on the planet resided in his home. The walls radiated warmth, generated from a family that enjoyed each other's company and delighted in each other's well being. All times of the day, laughter drifted throughout the snug little house. Singing and storytelling supplemented the evening meals.

The affection was so strong that it drew in Joseph's unmarried sister. Although she had a room of her own in Elder John's grand house, Caroline preferred to spend time in her younger brother's home with his daughters.

The girls, now ages eleven, ten, nine, six and five lived as a floral arrangement. Joy played the sunflower, breaking out with gladness, Hope favored the orchid, mysterious and infinite, Rose embodied the delicate, indomitable rose. Faith embraced vibrant green leaves that wrapped the bouquet, and Grace interspersed among them as sweet light blue baby's breath. Each possessed unique beauty, but in their together-ness the sisters dazzled brilliantly.

You never saw one without the other. Calling one equated to calling the five, because they all came running. The girls rallied together to meet the demands of farm life. They enthusias-tically carried out the chores. The sooner they finished the farm work, the sooner they could entertain each other.

The sisters shared clothes, kept each others' secrets and slept five in one bed. And although their daughters experienced harmony, Joseph and Isabel worried that as they grew older, the girls would need their own space. The couple wanted to build a larger house before their charming home lost its charm.

Joseph only wanted three acres of the three hundred-plus acreage ranch and farm for his growing brood. He asked for an acre for a home and play area and two acres to isolate the family from the cattle, which didn't always smell pleasant.

It required sacrificing some of the land earmarked for cattle grazing. Elder John denied the request. Doing that amounted to less room for six cattle. With the precarious nature of raising cattle — infancy death, disease or predators — he judged it as risky business. Elder John couldn't buy into sacrificing profits for human comfort.

Instead, he told Joseph the two oldest girls could live with his family in the Big House.

Joseph didn't like the idea, since it would place too much distance between the girls who would only see each other during farm duty and school and on Sundays when all the families came together for worship service and dinner in the Big House.

Joseph dreaded the day when he would have to separate his daughters.

13

Life on the ranch and farm went the way of sowing and reaping. Monday through Saturday unfolded with planting seeds, weeding the fields and harvesting the crops, depending on the season. The Lord commanded center of attention on Sundays.

Dawn found the families at the breakfast table as the wives rose with the roosters to prepare the first meal of the day. After breakfast, the men and children headed to the fields. The women kept the homes and cooked the meals.

At high noon, the hottest part of the day, the children left the fields for lunch and two hours of schooling. After reading, writing and arithmetic, the children resumed their farming chores. Snatching thirty minutes or so before dinner, leisure time didn't amount to much.

Joseph's daughters found respite and wonderment in the tales spun by Hope. Every morning upon awakening, the sisters eagerly waited to hear what fantasies had entertained Sister Number Two the night before.

The girls especially loved stories of a way of life where people didn't have to grow food and cattle and pigs didn't have to be slaughtered. Food would just appear with a mere thought.

Joy, Hope, Rose, Faith and Grace loved the idea of not having to work or kill to survive. Living all their lives on a farm and ranch, the sisters should have been used to hard work and sacrifice. But they weren't, especially when the cows and pigs lost their lives. The girls understood the food chain, yet it still hurt to lose the animals that they considered family.

In Hope's imaginary world, the people didn't want for anything. Needs were met before you knew you had one. A glass of water would appear on the table signaling time to drink. Rain would fall when the ground was dry, and gifts would appear under trees.

Instead of working from dawn to dusk, the occupants of Hope's dreams utilized time however they pleased. Social affairs with dancing and feasting topped many agendas. Folks with the most delicious and savory thoughts answered the call to prepare the buffet spread.

The people also enjoyed expressing themselves through art. They poured their inner selves on to canvases and into books with feelings of love, beauty and gratitude for the state of things.

In this universe, they sang and danced at a whim. Any day of the week, angelic voices could be heard harmonizing in homes and the jubilation spilled over into the streets with dancing as people's spirits freely soared.

Picnicking families and people without a care in the world populated the parks daily. One man stayed all day in the park sitting on a tree branch dangling his legs because he loved the view. He didn't want anything else in life but to watch the grass grow. The Richardson men, whose name symbolized power and bravery, would have branded him a yellow-bellied sapsucker dodging hard work and conquest.

Striking clothing drew the girls into Hope's dreams. Accustomed to functional wardrobes of denim overalls and bland cotton dresses, the sisters were awestruck to learn that clothing had other purposes than just covering for the body.

Made with all types of material and fabrics, clothes testified to the wearer's creativity. The phrase Sunday's best had no reference in this kingdom. Everyday wardrobes included people wrapped in ivory pearls, flowing vines or feathers that rivaled the peacock. Their outfits were limited only by their imaginations. If you could see it, you could wear it.

No one would be shocked to see a woman dressed suitably for a King's coronation, strolling down the street on a Monday afternoon with nowhere in particular to go.

In the stories, Rose fashioned herself a dress made of red and pink soft rose petals. Everyone would say, "ah, there goes Rose" as she left a sweet scent in her trails.

"If I lived there I would wear gold silk every day," chimed in Joy. "Except in the summer. Too hot. You'd sweat all over the place and the silk would stick like paste."

"Oh, but they do wear silk year-round," Hope added. "They just think of cooler days and so it is."

"Could we really control the weather?" wondered the sisters. Governing the climate would make life so much easier. No droughts, hurricanes, tornadoes, floods or lighting strikes to spoil their harvest.

Some dreams were more real and relevant than others. Family members led the cast of characters in these scenarios. Nonetheless, they were still taken for fantasy.

Hope envisioned her aunt capturing the heart of a farmer from a neighboring town. Aunt Caroline caught his attention when he came to the farm to talk trade with Elder John. He returned with a wagon full of seed that he promised in exchange for a calf. He also brought along flowers for his heart's sake.

Having never been wooed, the girls' aunt was uncomfortable with the attention. Her uneasiness was intensified by the fact that she was twelve years older than the smitten farmer, so she outright refused the young man's flowers.

Like a best-selling romance novel, his love would not be denied. The farmer showed up daily with gifts, flowers, candy, even a basket of chicks, until Aunt Caroline accepted his affections. They married and had three children, two boys and a girl.

When told of Hope's view of her future, the beloved aunt had no interest in the musings of a pre-adolescent, hormonal girl. Even Hope's sisters reserved their glee over the idea of a Prince Charming for Aunt Caroline. The fairy tale lacked plausibility.

While their aunt possessed fair features and an agreeable temperament, she was born with a club foot, a condition that frightened suitors. With one foot three inches shorter than the other, they questioned what else might be wrong with her biology?

Besides, at the age of thirty-three, Aunt Caroline had entered spinsterhood. Her aspirations reached as high as marrying a widower who needed help raising his offspring, never the prospect of romance and birthing children of her own. Aunt Caroline, a bride with child, was only in Hope's imagination.

In another one of Hope's dreams, her cousin Paul, Elder John's youngest son, left the farm to sail around the world. That too was chalked up to make-believe.

All the men in the family were born and died on the land. No one ever left. It was understood that the land belonged to the family and the family belonged to the land.

14

One particular morning, Hope arose hours before normal. She didn't awake with glossy eyes from mesmerizing sleep. Hope leaped forth with wakefulness as if she had discovered a hidden treasure.

"Sisters, sisters, sisters, get up," she said with a sense of destiny.

"What is it, Hope?" mumbled the groggy sisters who had been awakened way too early.

"We have a home of our own with enough rooms for all of us," Hope said.

"What?" quizzed the sisters as they wiped the sleep from their eyes.

"Our home, I was there!" exclaimed Hope.

"You dreamt we had a house?" questioned the sisters still under the influence of slumber.

"It wasn't a dream. I was there. It's green," she said as if still standing in front of the house.

"The color of the house is a soft grayish green. It has three levels. The first level has a flat roof that covers the porch. There are three windows trimmed in white paint that belong to three bedrooms, and our rooms are on the second level. The roof rises up to heaven like the steeple of a church but not as tall and it's wider. There is a window in the roof for Daddy and Mommy's bedroom."

The drowsy girls didn't say a word. Not that Hope would have been aware if they had. The house had seized her mind.

"The porch is broad and wraps all around the house, two porches, front and back. On the front porch are three white pillars holding up the flat roof. There are stairs leading up to the porch. One, two... seven stairs," she counted.

"I walk up to the porch and on my right is a white swinging bench hanging from the roof. I didn't see the swing when I was standing in front of the house because of the huge oak tree in the yard."

The fog of sleep started to leave the girls and Hope captured their full attention.

"The front door is wide open. I know we're not to enter other people's homes uninvited, so I call out, 'Anybody home?' I don't see anyone, but something just tells me to go inside, so I do.

"I hear the wood floors crack as I step in. The floor is a deep, dark red, looking sweeter than ripe cherries. The front room has a large couch and a big comfy-looking chair. In the corner is a piano. Mommy's Pink Lilies painting hangs on a wall. Did she sell it to the owners of the house, I wonder? Coming from the kitchen I smell the lavender that Mommy puts in the special soap that she sells.

"Behind the front room is the eating area. There is a table set for eight people. On it is a glass of something cool to drink. I am thirsty. I look around, but no one is there. I take a drink. It's iced tea spiked with peaches, Daddy's favorite.

"There are stairs in the eating room. I go up to the second floor where I find the bedrooms. The first room I enter is a small room with a bed. Next to the bed is a stand with a phonograph on it. The rug on the floor is worn with lots of grooves in it.

"In a larger room there are two beds. Balloons hang over one of the beds. Next to the other bed is a globe of the world. The third room also has two beds. A picture of a flying phoenix is posted on the wall facing one of the beds. Dream catchers with multi-colors hang over the other bed and it has a pillow with the words 'Sweet Dreams.'

"My heart starts pounding louder when I see that pillow. And that's when I knew. The painting of the lilies, the soap, Daddy's iced tea, dream catchers .... This was our house. I pick up the pillow and hold it close to my heart. We have our own home!

"And then I came back here."

The girls lived tighter than a sealed lid on a jar of preserves, not even air could penetrate them. The five of them shared a room barely large enough to hold two cows and a stack of hay.

They knew Elder John would never give up land so they could spread out. They also knew of his solution to have Joy and Hope move into his house. With a more powerful desire to be together, they muffled dreams of having a bed of their own and space to express their individuality.

They never pushed back when one person's elbow wound up in another's eye during restless sleep. Their parents never heard how the summer's heat turned the room into a pressure cooker.

They didn't even grumble amongst themselves. Grace never knew she snored, nor was Faith, who had unusually large feet, aware that the girls felt her shoes and boots took up more than their share of space in the crammed quarters.

Rose had no indication that her sisters didn't appreciate her turning their room into a sanctuary for ailing wildlife. They kept quiet her secret penchant for nursing injured rabbits and birds back to health. Not even the abandoned wolf cub that whimpered through the night for days could crack them.

But now they decided to speak.

Hope had broken the silence with talk of their home and own beds.   More than a tale to escape dullsville and cramped living conditions, the matter warranted earnest contemplation.

She didn't appear to be under the spell of an intoxicating dream. Hope spoke of things she knew. Her voice didn't betray any trace of fantasizing. Hope had always dreamt in colors, but now she heard the floors creak, smelled the lavender soap, tasted Daddy's tea and clutched the Sweet Dreams pillow. No castle in the sky, concluded the sisters, this was a home.

"The room with the raggedy rug is mine," said Joy who didn't need music to dance.

"Everyone knows me and the phoenix are kin," followed Rose.

"I am going to see the world," declared Faith.

"Waking up to balloons," beamed Grace, "every day is a party."

"We must tell Daddy," the girls concluded.

"A home with four bedrooms and a big sitting room, what do you say?" Joseph said. "Hope, you sure have the most amazing dreams."

"Daddy, it wasn't a dream. We really have such a house," Hope replied.

"Now girls, you know we don't have the land to build such a place," Joseph said.

"But Father, it already exists," the daughters said knowingly.

"Sweeties, we'll have such a home when donkeys fly," said Joseph dismissing his daughters. "Now go back to sleep and no more dreams about big fancy houses."

15

Faith couldn't hear the word no. The fourth sister had the fortitude to expect beyond reason, and was never hindered by lack of evidence or surmounting obstacles.

Her confidence surpassed that of an undefeated world class boxer. Call it the naiveté of childhood, but Faith believed she could do anything and acquire the desires of her heart and then some.

No matter how unbelievable, Faith clung to Hope's dreams as if they were ripe for plucking. Nothing Hope imagined stood out of reach.

She met every single male stranger that came by the farm with, "Excuse me mister, how old are you?"

Contrary to her mother's scolding, sassiness wasn't what prompted Faith's actions. She was simply alert for the man twelve years Aunt Caroline's junior who would marry her and father her three children.

Faith searched almanacs and collected articles on exotic places and world travels, looking for areas where the people didn't work and had the most favorable weather. As soon as she came of age, Faith planned to set out for that heaven on earth.

As an ardent disciple spreading the good news, she shared Hope's visions with her cousins.

"There's a world where people play all day. No work, nobody telling you what to do," said the believer. "We can eat whatever we want and never get sick. Have ice cream and cake for days straight and your tummy won't ache."

Jeers and mockery answered Faith's enthusiasm.

"You silly little girl, that's just make believe," taunted the chorus of her doubting cousins.

"Oh but there is such a place and I am going to move there when I grow up," Faith said. Looking to her cousin who had a promising future she continued, "Paul, you can find it with me. Hope dreamt that you will sail the world."

"I am not falling for that rubbish," responded Paul. "I was born a farmer's son and a farmer's son I will die."

"Not if you don't want to," Faith said. "Come with me and you can be whatever you want to be."

Her words seemed to sting Paul. How dare she defy his heritage?

"You're just a stupid girl who will believe any-thing anybody tells her," he lashed out and led his cousins in a round of:

Faith is a stupid girl,
A stupid girl, a stupid girl,
Faith is a stupid girl,
Who thinks she'll see the world.

Undaunted by their taunts, Faith picked up her grown-lady-sized feet and marched on.

Her cousins couldn't shake her, nor could her father's dismissive, "When donkeys fly."

"Why do you all look like someone burst your bubble?" Faith asked her sisters.

"Didn't you hear, Daddy? We're not moving," Hope said.

"But he didn't say no," Faith replied.

"Faith," laughed Joy, "when Daddy says 'when donkeys fly,' that's his way of saying it's never going to happen."

Don't challenge Faith; she could make the devil pray. Faith could outrun and jump all her cousins, including the teenage boys who were stunned when their little cousin could best them at arm-wrestling. The most talked about Faith-feat occurred when she went to help her older cousins with bear patrol.

Paul and Seth told their younger cousins that they had witnessed a bear attack on a hog. The ferocious creature snatched up the 150-pound pig and snapped it in two like a dried up twig.

None of the children could bear to think what would happen if bears crept upon them while working in the fields. The youngsters agreed to cover Paul and Seth's workload as they went on bear watch.

For two weeks the children took on the extra chores. They didn't mind. Paul and Seth had done an exceptional job of protecting them from being devoured by the wild animals. Not once had a bear come within sight.

Being stronger and faster than Paul and Seth, Faith reasoned her skills would be better used on bear patrol than weeding. Her cousins, both 15 years old and nearly men, objected, saying it was too dangerous for a six-year-old. But Faith didn't entertain their arguments. She waited about a half hour after the boys left for their watch and then set out on her own.

Faith didn't come across any bears. However, she did find Paul and Seth skinny dipping. No one knew for sure what happened next, but the boys came back black and blue and Faith told her sisters and cousins that from then on they would no longer be required to do Paul and Seth's share of the work.

The bear story defined Faith, a child who couldn't be intimidated by Goliath. The fact that donkeys don't fly didn't bully Faith into abandoning the family's new home.

"It will happen. We just have to get the donkey to fly," Faith said with determination.

"Little sister, flying donkeys, that's just abnormal," Hope said, proudly using the word that she had recently learned when the grownups were talking about the calf born with five legs.

Faith then reminded her sisters of their abnormalities.

"Joy, people are supposed to cry."

"Hope, people around here don't dream."

"Rose, babies born not breathing are dead."

"Grace, people don't get presents unless they earn them."

Her address of their characters helped the sisters see that they themselves were extraordinary and capable of the challenge. They agreed to teach the donkey to fly.

"We shouldn't have to perform tricks to get what we need," noted the youngest sister, who'd become accustomed to being ignored.

16

The Heir

"We really need to get the girls a dog," Joseph said as he peered through the window to see his daughters playing with the donkey.

Joy had taken up a game of fetch with the farm animal. She'd toss the stick and the donkey would chase after it. What a remarkable sight, the rigid legs of the old domestic ass springing across the field like a mustang. He moved as if he'd forgotten his pedigree.

Joseph didn't know that the children's play with the donkey had nothing to do with the need for a pet. Hope's dream home motivated the joyous interaction with the creature.

He told his daughters they would move when donkeys fly. But what does a donkey know about flying? Being uplifted, having the wind sweep through the body breaking all tethers to the earth. Can an animal who is weighted down know what it is to soar with the birds and greet the clouds? These things a work beast knew not.

Backbreaking labor, that a donkey understood all too well. Head hung low, nose to the ground, never looking up when plowing or hauling the weight of the world. A farm animal could write a book about it.

Joy reasoned if the donkey knew fun, he would want to fly and do other marvelous things as well. The sisters concurred and made the ass their new playmate.

Getting the donkey to partake in the activity of play proved to be more of a challenge than the girls assumed. When done with work, the farm animal only wanted to lie under the shade tree chewing grass.

When the sisters circled him with singing and dancing, the donkey dismissed them with a swat of his tail as if shooing away irritating flies.

Underestimating the persistence of his unwanted playmates, the ass soon discovered a smack of his tail couldn't deter the pestering humans. For weeks the girls ran around him chasing each other and giggling. They threw and kicked the ball over his head with no arousal from the donkey. Tuckered out from merriment, the girls would rest next to the creature as Hope told stories of Pegasus, the revered flying horse.

No one could tell a tale like Hope. She breathed

life into the fables of the mythical divine horse. The sisters could feel themselves on the back of Pegasus as he patrolled the skies. Their hearts raced with victory as the winged horse flew the girls into battle, slaying all doubts and resistance to their dream home.

Hope's animation also enchanted the donkey. His head rose from his grub, attention diverted from the emptiness of his existence. He locked his gaze upon Hope as she acted out Pegasus flying through the air with Zeus' lightning bolt.

"His speed streaked the skies with white heat and his power caused the heavens to roar with thunder," Hope said, arms flapping and twirling like a tornado about her sisters and the ass. "Glaciers gushed from the earth as his majestic hooves struck the ground."

With that the girls jumped up and started simulating flight and stomping their heels to draw water from the earth. "Pegasus, Pegasus, Pegasus," they chanted alternating between flying and stomping.

The donkey also rose and stared the sisters down. The beast didn't speak to the girls, but his eyes said, "See I am not just a dumb animal here to do grunt work. I am the heir to my cousin Pegasus and his glory. The Heir I am."

The sisters couldn't interpret the donkey's thoughts, but the intensity of his eyes told the girls to run. Faster than a flying horse, they bolted for the house seventy-five yards away. The farm animal gave chase. He soon became winded and collapsed.

Slower and less powerful than their cousin the horse, donkeys can only gallop for a short period. Heaving and puffing like someone in the throes of an asthma attack, the ass laid on the ground. He felt a calmness enter his bulky body as a hand stroked his throbbing back. Rose, the resurrected one, stroked him.

"Don't worry donkey, I was born not breathing," Rose said comforting the worn-out beast. "You'll catch up with us."

17

Stormy weather had new significance for the donkey after Hope's tales.

Before he sought shelter in the barn with the other animals, now he pranced about in the downpour. With each lightning strike, The Heir galloped more jubilantly, knowing that his ancestry carried the light.

On calm, starry evenings, the donkey could be seen looking up, searching the dark skies for his cousin Pegasus.

"That donkey has gone mad," Joseph said as he saw it running around in the rain storm. "I knew something was wrong with that beast. It was in the way he pulled the cart, stepping like he was high and mighty and shaking his head like he had a luxurious mane. And he's always looking up. Maybe he's got that old person's disease."

The farm animal hadn't gone mad. He had been infected by Hope. Tales of Pegasus sparked new life in the aged donkey, which inhabited space long before the time of Joseph.

Fueled with destiny, The Heir soon began chasing the sisters around until they all became drunk on silliness. Smooth laughter replaced his nagging bray. No longer collapsing as the sisters ran him, the donkey looked forward to the sweet tiredness after his daily workload.

Running after the girls required the donkey to change directions without hesitation. He had to move like a racehorse in its prime, instead of a lumbering old, overworked animal. With the girls darting about him calling out "here donkey," The Heir started, stopped and turned quickly, maneuvering like a lion hunting gazelle.

Getting the donkey to jump would be the formidable obstacle for the sisters. Flying required him to loosen his grip on stability, letting his feet leave sure ground.

Giggling and laughing, the sisters hopped back and forth over the five-foot fence separating Joseph's land from the grazing fields, hoping The Heir would follow.

The sound of excitement drew out wild rabbits who wanted to play. A half dozen or so airborne rabbits cleared the fence effortlessly. Their long floppy ears resembled wings as they glided in the air.

"Now they're playing with those pesky rabbits!" exclaimed Joseph from his kitchen window view.

The girls had springing rabbits, but no jumping donkey. Not influenced by the levity, The Heir remained grounded.

Unbeknownst to the sisters, the donkey, a cautious creature, would not put itself in harm's way. When they tried to coax him over the five-foot fence, he wouldn't budge.

"Maybe he just needs a push," reasoned the children.

Rallying around the animal, they pushed and pulled with all their might. A strong sense of survival set in. Even the name Pegasus lost its lure. Possessing an immeasurable stubbornness, the donkey dug in like a two-ton boulder being pushed up a hill.

When that didn't work, the girls tried to entice the creature over the fence with ginger biscuits, his favorite. Grace would give The Heir a treat, even though he hadn't attempted to clear the hurdle.

"Grace, don't do that," scolded her sisters. "We'll never get him to move his hind legs if you reward him."

"I can give him a biscuit if I want to," pouted Grace.

"Don't you get it, Grace, grownups make people do what they want them to do by giving them things," the girls said. "Donkeys don't just fly on their own; we have to make them fly."

"We're not grownups," Grace said. "And we're not the boss of donkey."

"Grace be quiet, we're going to make this donkey fly," said the sisters as they pushed and pulled, trying to haul the donkey over the fence.

"This isn't fun anymore," Joy said and for the first time in her life it sounded as if she were whining.

"Maybe dreams are just dreams," Hope followed.

"No!" rose up from the gut of Rose, "Dreams are real. We're not dead yet."

"We just need to believe more and work harder," added Faith. "This donkey will fly. We have to want it bad enough."

So the girls mustered up all their strength and prayers and once again tried to push and pull the animal over the fence.

Still the ass sat.

In Grace's eyes, the problem had nothing to do with the donkey refusing to jump. She didn't comprehend why her sisters felt they had to produce a miracle for something that they already possessed.

Just as an orange seed is buried in fertile ground, life was planted in Hope with the dream of the family's new home. No one had to do anything to make the seed into fruit. Without coaxing and prodding, the sun shined, rain fell, roots sprouted, buds appeared, oranges ripened.

Grace understood that life had already given the sisters their dream home. They simply needed to nurture the house in their hearts and watch it come forth.

"Just stop, we don't have to struggle," Grace said as her sisters fumed with frustration. "We already have all that we need."

For the first time they actually heard the youngest daughter. But the sisters were too tired to bicker. In exasperation, they all fell asleep with Grace's words hanging overhead, whispering in their ears.

"We don't have to struggle; we already have all that we need."

The sweetest, invigorating sleep came upon all five girls. From the soles of their feet to the crowns of their heads, they felt the currents of energy that bloomed flowers, sparked diamonds, stilled troubled waters.

18

The sky above was crystal clear and bright blue, nothing but glorious beauty on the horizon. No clouds, no threatening weather, which meant that billowing dark spot over the border of the grazing fields near Joseph's home could only be one thing.

_F I R E!!!!!!!!!!!!_

The family dashed into the fire drill. They urgently filled barrels with water and loaded them on wagons. Without hesitation the Richardsons then donned stomping boots and gathered heavy burlap sacks for suffocating flames.

Ready for battle, men, women and children, piled in wagons and raced toward the impending doom.

19

The sound of the commotion drew the girls out of their peaceful sleep.

As they awoke, the sisters saw a structure standing about a hundred yards away in the grazing fields.

"How long have we been asleep?" they wondered because only cattle occupied the fields when they slipped themselves into unconsciousness.

As she shook off the sleep and the structure came into clearer view, it became evident to Hope, "Sisters, it's our house!"

"What!" screamed the girls, who jumped to their feet, hurtled the fence and sprinted toward the house.

The Heir had also risen. The sight of a strange white horse running through the fields moved the donkey. Without trepidation, he too cleared the fence in pursuit of the stallion whose thick flowing mane parted like wings as it galloped.

As the sisters made their way into the house, The Heir caught up with the white horse, which glided with lightning speed. This close to the intriguing stallion, the donkey could see it had blue piercing eyes. They exchanged glances.

Although The Heir had never seen the horse around the farm, he sensed familiarity. Like long-lost kin reunited, the two animals triumphantly raced around and around and around the house, generating enough heat to melt the earth.

20

When the rescue crew arrived to the spot of the smoke, it found Joseph, Isabel and Caroline in the field, but no fire. Riveted to the black cloud, the three stood like statues with eyes heaven-bound. The circling dark mass was a mystery. Remnants of grayish streams floated from the earth to the heavens, indicating where the circle originated, but nothing more.

The ground in the area showed no signs of a burning, just green grass glistening with fresh morning dew, which was strange, given that it was almost dinner time. Other than that, nothing else seemed out of the ordinary.

Despite their best attempts, the family couldn't conjure a reasonable explanation for the mysterious cloud. They grasped for answers.

Could it be one of those flying machines that had had the world abuzz?

The family had heard of two brothers flying in a machine. Only a few claimed to have witnessed the flights and many believed the story to be a hoax.

Brought up on practicality, the Richardsons sided with those who didn't believe in the possibility of man navigating his way through the skies. Their forefathers didn't entertain abstract thoughts and taught their progeny to ally with nature, that which is concrete and bears fruit.

"Can't be those flying brothers," reasoned the group. Flying machines weren't natural and in all his genius, man would never break the laws of God.

While the family speculated, the blackness began to dissipate and what appeared before their eyes ranked more far-fetched than talk of men flying in machines.

A donkey, Joseph's ass drifted in the sky. The same donkey that plowed and ate dirt all its life had dared nature and taken flight.

In all the excitement, the families didn't notice that Joseph's five daughters were missing. However, they didn't need to look very far for Joy, Hope, Rose, Faith and Grace.

21

Unrestrained electricity reverberated off the walls as five screaming girls raced through the house claiming their rooms.

Grace bounced upon her bed, leaping higher than an Olympic pole vaulter as she tried to grab the balloons hanging overhead. Faith feverishly spun her globe, searching for the place where people didn't work and food appeared with a mere thought. In her room, Rose soared high like the phoenix.

Twirling the dream catcher, Hope moved about her room as if performing a ceremonial dance to bring forth other dreams. Another groove formed in the rug as Joy waltzed in her room.

Jubilance ran high in the wood-frame structure, causing the house to rattle with delight. The foundation shook like an earthquake registering an eight on the Richter scale. The girls fell through the ceiling of the first level.

When the dust settled, the sisters found themselves right where they started, on the ground behind the fence separating their barn house from the grazing cattle. The family's new home had vanished.

The sisters surmised that somehow Hope had transported them into her dream. After all they slept so tightly together as one body, perhaps they could have had one mind, one dream.

Now the giddy mob that descended upon them made no sense at all.

"*I shall marry!*"

"*I am a sailor!*"

"*I am the minister of this family!*"

"*I want to teach!*"

"*I want to sing!*"

"*I want to drive the cattle!*"

"*My husband will have a son!*"

"Daddy, daddy, daddy," screamed the girls as they were being crushed by hugs and kisses.

"Here I am darlings," said Joseph as he and Isabel pushed their way through ecstatic relatives to reach their daughters.

"What is the matter with everyone?" asked the perplexed girls.

"Darlings, they're just overcome with awe after seeing the donkey fly," Joseph said.

"The donkey flew," screamed the girls as they turned to look at The Heir, who continued to sit on his rump, looking like an ordinary farm animal.

"And we missed it," added the girls, sounding dejected.

"Missed it, girls you were flying on the donkey," Joseph said recounting the miraculous event. "Joy and Hope were on his back, Rose and Faith were dangling from the sides and Grace was holding on by the tail."

"No Daddy, we tried but the donkey wouldn't move," said the sisters as tears of lost hope streamed down their faces. "It was all just a dream."

"No," Joseph said hugging the girls. "You were flying and we all saw it."

By that time Elder John made his way to the front of the crowd.

"Joseph, we'll build you a house, right there," he said pointing to the spot where they saw The Heir and the girls flying. "You can have all the land you want."

The girls' sobs were silenced. Indeed, the donkey flew that day.

Epilogue - Your Story

The Day the Donkey Flew is the tale of your destiny. Within you are marvelous dreams that will make the world an amazing place — if only you will allow them to come forth.

As demonstrated by our friend the donkey, you must look beyond overwhelming circumstances and realize your own potential. You are The Heir to greatness. Journey inside and discover the hidden jewels. Who knows what lies within? Maybe it's the masterpiece of this century, or perhaps it's the key to immortality.

Note that in the story, the donkey named himself The Heir. No one can name you, define who you are or chart your future. Only you know what's buried deep within you and ready to be released. Only you can determine what contributions you'll make to this cosmic celebration called Life.

You appear to be grounded, but nothing can prevent you from taking flight.

Your Resources

Joy makes donkeys want to fly.

Hope makes donkeys believe they can fly.

Rose lifts donkeys when they fall from the sky.

Faith empowers donkeys to fly.

Grace flies donkeys.

Go play! Allow Joy to show you the bliss of life. The Universe is looking for a playmate. Soar with eagles, swim with dolphins, sing with crickets, and skip with squirrels.

Joy fosters inspiration. Hope awakens.

"What else is possible," she asks? "We don't have to live as our ancestors. We have our own home, our own legacy."

You try to silence Hope with doubt and limitations. You tell her "when donkeys fly."

Forget about what you tried before that didn't work. Disregard failure. Meet Rose, the resurrected one. Born dead, she rose. Get up, and try again.

Oh, but you've already made your fame and fortune. You say you've seen it all. "Been there, done that," you boast.

Great, then do some more! Don't allow success to trap you into complacency. The Richardson Family was satisfied with living on its inheritance, yesterday's glory.

Life is constantly evolving, unfolding. What worked yesterday, doesn't work today. The Universe re-births itself daily.

It's never too late; you're never too old. There are infinite ideas to be explored.

"But it's never been done before," you might protest.

If it had, then it wouldn't be revolutionary. Besides, it was given you to do. Only you can do what is yours to do.

Have a talk with Faith. She says "yes" to ideas that have not yet manifested, and she ignores those who would limit and deny the sublime.

Faith is not intimidated by what has never been done before. Nor is Faith deterred by taunts and mockery. The Wright Brothers were ridiculed. Their hometown newspaper refused to print their first accomplishments of flight and a headline in the international press read "Flyers or Liars." Faith kept them focused despite the media.

Your Dream

Faith talked you into taking on the dream. You've read every self-help book, hired a life coach, done all that you can and that donkey still won't fly. Now you want to quit.

Don't walk away from your dream, but do release it. Give it back to the Universe. Rest from your efforts, and watch as Grace takes over.

Soon the donkey will be flying and you'll see the world from new heights. It is a wonderful place.

"Oh Wow!" will become the song of your heart as the Universe rejoices with you.

Insights and Questions

I hope *The Day the Donkey Flew* has encouraged you to reevaluate your dreams and talents and ponder your existence and destiny. With this in mind, I offer the following insights and questions to drive you deeper within.

1. Why was Joy born first?

2. Isabel had the ability to dream, but lost it due to self-doubt and her desire to deliver a male heir. Hope is a clear channel, having no worldly dreams or nightmares.
Can you suspend your adult sensibilities and allow childlike wonderment?

3. Hopelessness is often masked as laziness. After farm work, the donkey only wanted to lie underneath the tree and chew grass. People don't move because they don't have a vision: they become complacent, accept the status quo. They lack the energy to do anything else

because they have no inspiration. Hope has not yet awakened. When you are motivated by a vision, you can work all day and still find yourself charged with energy to tend to the dream.

Is it laziness or hopelessness that has you bound? What is your source of inspiration?

4. Rose represents the resurrection, our ability to start over again. Forgiveness is her power. We must be willing to forgive ourselves and others before we can move forward. We must also be willing to surrender our current success. Sometimes it's not the bad, but the good that grounds us.

What must you release in order to take off?

5. Faith allows us to say "yes" to our divine heritage. With Faith, we are steadfast and do not waiver in our convictions. However, she can be rigid and unyielding.

The Day the Donkey Flew wasn't the story I was planning to tell. For the past decade, I've been writing a novel. I would start then stop and start then stop, going back and forth and never reaching a steady flow. I also had the idea to write a series of poems about five sisters, Joy, Hope, Rose, Faith and Grace. Again, the words just weren't flowing. Then one day *The Day the Donkey Flew* came pouring out.

I had to put aside the novel and the poems and allow *The Day the Donkey Flew* to unfold. I didn't lose faith, but was flexible enough to change directions. Sometimes we shun our gifts because they are not what we expected. In *The Day the Donkey Flew*, Joseph wanted a son, but he received what he needed, the gift of Joy, Hope, Rose, Faith and Grace.

Faith can also be argumentative and dog-matic. She likes taunting the devil, getting us into unnecessary challenges. Did Faith really have to beat up her cousins?

Do you recognize when you are being faithful or obstinate?

6. Grace is the unifying force. She harmonizes Joy, Hope, Rose and Faith. There is no more pushing and pulling, just the reign of Spirit.

Do you know when to let and go and allow Grace to takeover?

Special Acknowledgment

Every idea has a support system that provides structure, sustenance, significance and satisfaction. I acknowledge my support.

For their unconditional love and for just being a part of my experience, I thank my husband Ryan, our sons Andrew, Ryan Jr., Antonio, Elisha, and our daughters, Danicka and Davenja. I trust that my brother, Irving Newsome; my uncles, Charles and Herman Benyard; aunts, Joevelyn Durham, Glendora Meyers and Valerie Pettygrue; and my in-laws, nieces, nephews and cousins know that my life has been enriched by their presence.

I am grateful to have people who have embraced me as part of their family. Ernestine Williams, Keith Allen, Dr. Barbara Cobb, Davia Laswell, Baird Cobb, and Elizabeth Allick have all treated me as kin. My godparents Joseph and Janephine Chaney and god sisters Karole Mingle-McCray, Jennifer Mingle-Smith and the late Sybil L. Mingle always believed I shared their blood. And then there are the sons and daughter that I didn't birth, but who are nevertheless mine, Victoria Lecorps, Winston Lee Jr.,

Bevon Woodroffe, Troy Jeffery, Albie Evans and Jeremy Tye, Sr.

The gift of friendship is something I deeply cherish and I have been blessed to call many wonderful people my friends. I wish to acknowledge those dear friends who have encouraged me to live my dreams. Thanks abound to Layla Carroll Hicks, Norma and Margaret Cox, Patrick Michel, Tamian Wood, Sirvonne Carmicheal, Keith C. Wade, Jennifer Chee Bravo, Edith Torres, Lilian Bohorquez, Yvonne Mccormack-Lyons, Richa Tripathi Mishra, Ben Thacker, Peter Dooling, Ruben Perez, Florence Moss, Irene Berry, Germaine Tilney, Jef Morris, Tony Garcia, Wyatt Payne, Ernie Capers, Daniel Montanha and Wei Lun Huang.

I also acknowledge my Tai Chi Community (teachers, students and colleagues) and The Novellettes (Barbara Knaubb, Dr. Barbara Cobb, Emily Davis, Tracy Sherman, Julia Malakoff, Sheila Kelly, Marilyn Polin, and Leslie Sevastopoulos) for the inspiration generated whenever we are together.

The Production Team

I thank my marketing team, Andrew Lee and Laura Boman, for wholeheartedly embracing the project. Graphic designer Tamian Wood merits gratitude not only for her design talents, but her impeccable skills as a beta-reader. I felt the jubilation of a mother giving birth as illustrator Shift Wood gave form to each character. Megan Peterson's thoughtful and thorough editing made working with her a joyful experience. Ernestine Williams is not only the copyreader, but she is also my heart.

My Journalism Teachers

Alice Klement, my journalism teacher at the University of Miami, deserves applause for showing her students that the field of reporting could be a playground and for allowing them to play.

There are teachers who inspire and those who irritate. My Carol City Senior High School journalism teacher Dr. Joyce Annunziata did both. She fostered my love of writing, but I was frightened by her expectations.

Dr. Annunziata, I now believe in flying donkeys.

About the Author

Elisa C. Newsome Smith is a former journalist and communication executive living in South Miami, Florida. Her passion for writing and storytelling is now expressed through poetry and fiction. This is her first literary publication.

It was her spirit of Joy, Hope, Rose, Faith and Grace that enabled Elisa to leave a prosperous career and live her new dreams, which included forming Abide in Chi, a company that empowers people to release their radiance through the practices of Tai Chi, Qigong and Massage Therapy.

Her desire to help others connect with their inner bliss continues to evolve as she developed Elisa's Playshop, a place where inspiration flows freely. Through uplifting and soul-searching literature and activities that foster creativity, Elisa's Playshop seeks to leave people lighthearted and filled with admiration and inspiration. Visit her at www.elisasplayshop.com or www.facebook.com/elisasplayshop.

About the Artists

Illustration by Shift Wood

Shift Wood is an aspiring artist living in Chandler, Arizona. In the first grade, he entered an art contest, which began a life-long love affair with artistic expression.

As a young adult, Shift began to paint graffiti murals for various organizations. Currently a tattoo artist, his love for art continues to grow as he explores a multitude of mediums, including pen, pencil, watercolor and oil and acrylic paint.

Cover design and interior layout by Tamian Wood

Tamian Wood is a graphic designer, currently based out of sunny South Florida. Using art, photography, typography and digital collage techniques, she creates book covers that appeal to the eye and the mind, to entice the book browser to become a book reader. She holds degrees in computer science and graphic design, is the winner of numerous design awards and a proud member of Phi Theta Kappa National Honour Society.